CATS'
WHISKERS

Written by Janet McLean
Illustrated by Andrew McLean

A LITTLE ARK BOOK

ALLEN & UNWIN

THE CATS

Here they are. . .

Pssst!

Max and Minerva,

Monica,

they used to be kittens

born in an alley

Lin,

Roly,

and Jake.

ASTIR

Here are the cats,
getting ready. . .

'There's Jake.'

stretching, yawning,
bumping heads to say
'Good morning',

odd socks

wash my back, please

combing, cleaning,
primping, preening.

'Monica, you have to
stay inside today.'

'Don't be scared, Jake.'

WATCHING & WAITING

Here are the cats,
all eyes and ears...

gazing at goldfish,

glaring through glass,

looking out for a mouse hiding inside its house,

grrrrowl!

and stubbornly staring from stairs.

'Mm'rowww! Come out, Monica!'

oops!

Here are the cats,
snooping around. . .

pawing a mouse hole,
inspecting a bag,
exploring a trolley that's full,

sniffing about to find a way out, and tugging a piece of red wool.

'No! Monica!!'

'Here, Jake. I'm your friend.'

Here are the cats,
climbing and clamouring...

'Where's Monica?'

Woof!

playing around
high up in a tree,

'Come through, Jake.'

a balancing-act cat

a cat cacophony

'Hist! Get off my roof, Max!'

prowling the roof tops where no one can see.

'Brr'oww! Hello, Jake.'   'Mmm'roww! Hello, Monica.'

Max had a narrow escape.

STEALTHY

here boy!

Here are the cats,
furtive and sly...

creeping along to sneak up on a bird,

stealthily stalking his prey,

cat burglar

Shh!

waiting to ambush a dog passing by,
and quietly slinking away.

In and out the chimney pots.

Together at last.

POUNCING

Here is a gleeful cat...

swooping on a mouse.

TOPSY-TURVY

Here are the cats,
upside down and downside up...

friskily frolicking,
romping and rollicking,

twisting and twirling,
wriggling and whirling.

'Have a drink, Jake.'

'Too fat, Monica!'

ANNOYING

Here are the pesky cats...

knocking down knick-knacks,
miaowing for food,
all tangled up underfoot,

wanting to come in...   go out...   come in...   go out,
unfussed, and staying put.

'Monica! Bedtime!'

HUNGRY

Here are the cats, always peckish...

patiently waiting for tidbits to drop,

snaffling pieces of cake,

'You can come in, Jake.'

Mi-aaaaow

stealing a sausage and scoffing it down,
then nursing a big tummy ache.

'Monica! It's your favourite – cream cake.'

CONTENTED

Here are the cats,

in their favourite places. . .

wedged between chimneypots,

sprawled in the sun,

asleep on the narrowest ledge,

not Grandpa's hat!

'Where are you, Monica?'

snoozing in smelly socks,

waiting on the mail box,

and lazing about in a hedge.

She's hiding.

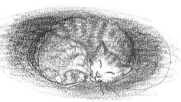

CRAZY

Here are the cats,
raising a ruckus...

Max's bath
time.

suddenly scampering, skittering, scurrying,
and cleverly looping the loop.

'I can't find Monica anywhere.'

Minerva always lands on her feet.

Lin looping loops.

She's still hiding.

CATASTROPHE

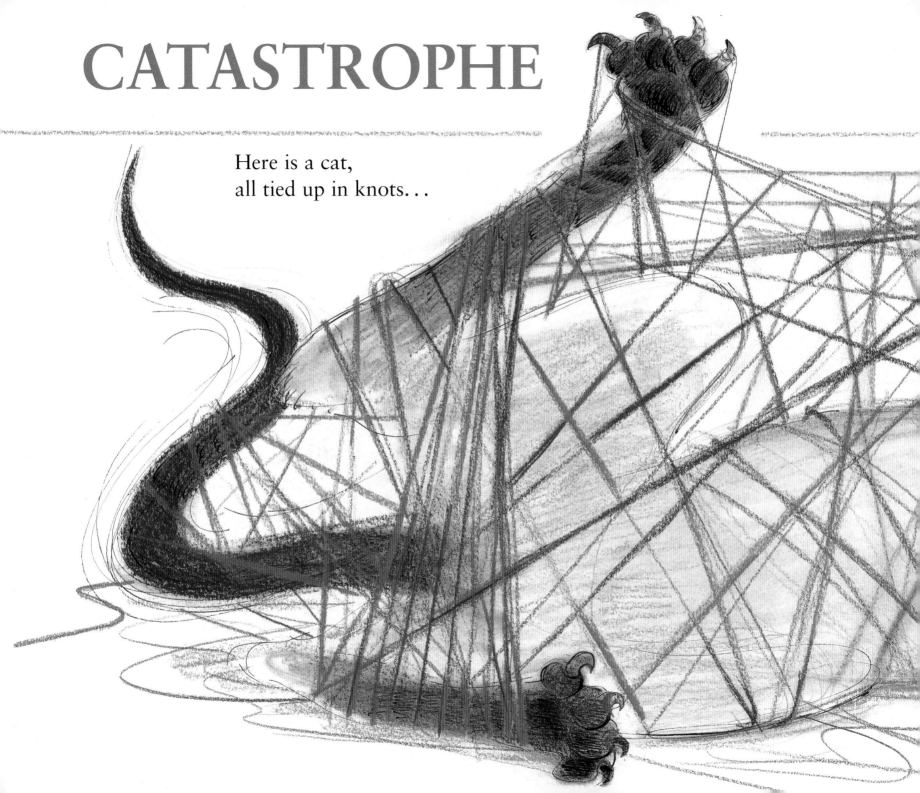

Here is a cat,
all tied up in knots. . .

cat's cradle

MAKING FRIENDS

Here are the cats,
wanting to be where we are...

'Hello, Jake!'

cats in laps

cat hat

'What's that noise, Hamish?'

'Can you see anything?'

'Jake, you old smoocher.'

PURRING

Here is Monica,
found at last...

And look, she's had kittens!
One, two, three, four, five, six...
and little Jake makes seven.

CATS & KITTENS

Here they all are... Shhhh!

Max, Minerva, Lin and Roly...Monica and Jake...and their kittens.